44 Tiny Acrobats

Sylvia Bishop
Illustrated by Ashley King

LITTLE TIGER
LONDON

For my family, with love x
~ SB

For Sam and Liz, thank you for being the ultimate and inspiring friends with the warmest and biggest of hearts xx
~ AK

OUR FIRST ACT

The Incredible Unwanted Circus!

It was the first day of the Christmas holidays, and for Betsy Bow-Linnet and her grandad that meant it was Christmas Decorations Day. Grandad had got the boxes out of the cellar as usual, and started whistling Christmas tunes as usual; but something wasn't usual about him, and Betsy didn't know what was wrong.

"Let the mayhem begin, B," he said. He tucked some tinsel round his head. "First things first, we must decorate your old grandad.

How do I look?"

He was pretending to have fun, but Betsy wasn't fooled. Normally his elbows wafted merrily around when he talked, or moved, or breathed. Today they drooped at his sides like two sad worms in a cardigan. And if Grandad was only pretending to have fun, then Betsy couldn't really have fun either.

The only ones who *were* having fun were Betsy's forty-four African pygmy mice.

This was their first experience of Christmas decorations. Betsy and Grandad pulled out baubles and bells and bright pieces of ribbon, and each new treasure caused a wave of astonished squeaking and, unfortunately, nibbling. The mice were normally very well behaved, but ever since the cold winter weather had set in, some instinct had made them start eating everything in sight.

"Alas!" said Grandad, holding up a paper angel. "His heavenly foot hath been chewed. We might have to put the mice away, B."

"Oh no," said Betsy. "They get so sad if I keep them cooped up all day."

Grandad nodded. "A distraction then." He ferreted around in the decorations box and held up some old worms of tinsel. "How about they learn some acrobatics? We could hang these from the doorway for them."

This was a good idea. Betsy strung up the tinsel and showed the mice how to climb up and down and swing back and forth. It worked like a charm: they went scurrying around the colourful strands with squeaks of glee, while Betsy and Grandad got on with the decorations in peace.

Grandad kept up his determined whistling, but he didn't chatter away as usual, and he did everything just a bit too slowly. It felt as though he needed winding up again, like tired clockwork.

"Grandad," said Betsy at last. "Is everything al—?"

Grandad held up a wreath and examined it. "Ding dong merrily on *hiiiigh*," he sang, "a mouse has chewed this *hooolly*."

The mice innocently swung back and forth on their tinsel, whiskers akimbo.

"I just mean," said Betsy, "you seem a bit—"

"Ding dong verily oh *whyyyyyy*? Their insides can't feel *jooolly*!"

"Grandad," she tried once more. "Is there—"

But Grandad cut her off with a, "Back in a tick, B!" and went whistling off to hang the wreath on the door, elbows drooping sadly.

So Betsy went back to hanging tiny baubles on the hundreds of rare and exotic ferns that her mother filled the house with and tried to think what might be bothering him. Out of the corner of her eye, she kept watch on the mice. They had got so good at controlling the swing of the tinsel strands that they were now swinging them into complicated plaits.

This was not surprising. The mice were remarkably clever. When Betsy had first been given them, they had already been trained to play the piano. That's why there were forty-four of them: they each played two of the piano's eighty-eight notes, and they all had names like G-to-G-sharp-fourth-octave. Betsy had had to keep them a secret when they first arrived, and those forty-four tiny secrets had caused her a lot of trouble – but that's another story.

They weren't secrets now, and they could do much more than play the piano. Betsy had taught them lots of new tricks. They could jump through tiny hoops, and do cartwheels and paw-stands and star jumps, and draw pictures with inky paws and use a can-opener (if they all worked together and pushed very hard).

Betsy watched as D-flat-to-D-fifth-octave made an impressive leap between two bits of tinsel. B-to-C-second-octave tried to join in, but got confused and leaped on to a nearby fern instead. Betsy went to coax him off before he got round to nibbling it.

When Grandad came back in, he was still whistling stubbornly and he dodged all Betsy's concerned questions. Betsy sighed, and decided she would have to tell her parents about it, to see if they could get to the bottom of the problem.

It turned out that she didn't need to tell them. Somehow her parents already knew. When they arrived home ten minutes later, they were both armed with up-cheering things. Her mother, Bella, had brought a book of piano duets – she and Grandad were both excellent pianists and loved to play together. Her father, Bertram, was clutching a bulging bag of cream cakes (he had given up playing the piano these days, but was an excellent cream-cake eater, and he loved to eat them, with or without anybody else). And they had both brought enormous smiles and chirpy voices and ENTHUSIASM.

"I thought we could play a few duets together, Dad!" exclaimed Bella.

"An' I foughmff ee coulff haf afnoon tea," exclaimed Bertram, with his mouth full of an eclair that he was sampling, just to make sure it was all right.

Grandad tried to roll-his-eyes-and-wink at Betsy when the other two weren't looking, but his heart wasn't really in it. It ended up being more wobbling-his-eyes-and-squinting-a-bit.

Bella won the ENTHUSIASM contest and Grandad went off with her to play duets. Bertram looked at his cream cakes sadly. Then he realized something and cheered up at once. "Well, B," he said, opening the bag. "I guess these are all for you and me then."

Betsy looked at him, with his armful of up-cheering cakes. What did he know that she didn't? "Dad," she said. "What's wrong with Grandad?"

From above, a soft duet began. Bertram looked at Betsy kindly over his half-moon spectacles, and said, "Have you looked out of the window today, B? At the front?"

"No?"

"Come and see." So Betsy followed Bertram, dodging the swinging mice in the doorway, over to the bay window in the parlour. The Bow-Linnets lived in a London townhouse where Bertram had grown up, and although it was tired round the edges and a bit of a mess – mostly because of ferns and pianos and, of course, mice – it was quite grand, and had beautiful views. It looked across the road to a wide common, which was normally only occupied by a few dog walkers and a huddle of crows.

But today the far side of the common was a hive of activity. Somebody had put boards down over a large patch of grass and there were colourful vans parked everywhere, with FRY AND SONS written on the side. In among the vans, people were bustling about, laughing and calling to each other. Watching them, Betsy felt a strange sense of longing.

FRY
FRY and SONS'

"That," said Bertram, "is your grandma's circus."

Betsy did her best to turn off the sense of longing sharpish, because she absolutely did *not* want anything to do with Grandma's circus. When her mother Bella had been seven, Betsy's grandma Beryl had left her and Grandad to go back to her old circus life. She was a fabulous animal trainer, and performed with dogs and horses and other creatures under the name Gloria Sprightly – she even had mice like Betsy's, which had been her grandad's idea. She had died a little while ago, but Betsy had never met her. They hardly ever talked about it. The memories were too painful.

"It hasn't been in town since you were very small," said Bertram. "Just arrived today. Bit of a nasty shock for poor old Grandad."

Betsy could see that it must have been. She tried very hard to focus on the memory of Grandad's drooping elbows, and not to feel even a little bit excited as the bustling people began to lay a great tent over the ground and circle round it, ready to raise it up to full height.

"So," said Bertram, "we'll all just have to ignore it and be extra nice to Grandad. Your mother has tickets for you three to see a concert tonight, to take his mind off things – I wish I could come, but I have to go and see Great-Aunt Agatha." He turned a little pale as he said this. Bertram's great-aunt was a fearsome woman and his monthly dinners with her filled him with dread. "So," he said bravely, "can I count you in for Operation

Cheer-up-Grandad, B?"

Betsy nodded, and turned away from the excitement outside. The mice were now leaping between the tinsel strands in time to the soft piano music above, chirping blissfully.

But at that moment, F-to-F-sharp-first-octave leaped with a bit too much aplomb and not quite enough accuracy, and tumbled to the floor with a tiny, terrified *squeeooook*.

Betsy and Bertram stood frozen for a mouse-sized nanosecond, then rushed over, saying things like, "*Ohnoohnoohno!*" and, "*Pleasebeokpleasebeok!*" and, "*Ooooh!*" For a moment, the little comma of reddish-brown fur lay very still. But as they watched, he heaved a trembling breath and gathered himself on to his paws. Then he twitched all over, as though finding out what was still in the right place.

"He's OK," said Betsy, kneeling down to see. "He's OK." She held out the back of her hand and F-to-F-sharp-first-octave crawled on, dragging his right front leg. (You should *always* avoid picking up an African pygmy mouse. They are so small, they might get squashed.)

"Something a bit off with his paw, isn't there?" said Bertram, crouching alongside her. Betsy nodded.

Squeach, said the mouse sadly.

Betsy stroked him very gently, his spine a tiny string of beads under his fur, and tried to pull herself together. It was almost too much to have a sad grandad *and* an injured mouse on Christmas Decorations Day. But if she got upset too, then things were only going to get worse. So she just had to treat it like a messy room: roll up her sleeves and set about putting things right.

First, she would get the mouse to the vet's, because that's the best thing to do for a mouse with a painful paw. Then, she would find out what was best for a grandad with a painful memory and do that, whatever it was.

"I'll call the vet's," she said to Bertram.

"Yes, good idea," he said. "Poor little fellow."

The vet couldn't see them until six o'clock. Bertram would have left for his great-aunt's by then, so he suggested asking Bella to go with her, but Betsy wouldn't hear of it.

"Mum's got to take Grandad to the concert," she insisted. "The vet's is only on the other side of the common. I can go by myself. Looking after Grandad is more important."

"Don't worry, B, Grandad's all right really—" Bertram began. But then Grandad came down to make tea, singing the word 'tea' repeatedly to the tune of 'Jingle Bells'. Betsy and Bertram exchanged glances as he shuffled past them.

Grandad was brilliant at making up songs. "Tea tea tea, tea tea tea, jingle all the tea." was definitely not one of his best.

"Well, I don't know if you should really go on your own..." said Bertram.

"Oh what *teeeea* it is to tea in a one-horse open TEA! Oh bother," said Grandad. It was hard to be sure, but it sounded as if he might have walked into an unexpected door frame.

"OK," said Bertram. "Betsy on mouse duty, Mum on Grandad duty. And Dad on Great-Aunt duty, worst luck."

Bella wasn't sure about the plan at first, but when the common lit up with a sparkling FRY AND SONS sign, they all knew they *had* to get Grandad out of the house. The injured mouse was still squeaking gently to himself in pain, so there was no question of delay; and when it was suggested that Bertram could call Great-Aunt Agatha to cancel, he gave a very similar squeak.

So at ten to six, with strict instructions to

go-straight-to-the-vet's-and-straight-home-again-and-don't-answer-the-door-to-anyone-and-we'll-be-home-soon, it was Betsy alone who packed forty-four mice up into their case. She only needed F-to-F-sharp-first-octave, but as soon as she called the command, "Home!", all forty-four obediently came running.

"Well," said Betsy, "it's probably good to have you with him. For moral support."

One mouse blinked at her in a way that *might* have been supportive, but the rest were very busy trying to nibble the case. It was made of smart brown leather and divided into forty-four glass-fronted sections, each with a mouse's name. It was not even a little bit edible, but they were doing their best.

Betsy sighed, picked up the case and set off for the vet's. It was raining. This was officially the worst Christmas Decorations Day ever.

The vet was very excited to find that the mice were genuine African pygmy mice. When Betsy showed her how they could march in time and cartwheel and do star jumps and so on, she was very, *very* excited, and spent a lot longer examining F-to-F-sharp-first-octave than really seemed necessary. But eventually she decided it was just a sprain and bound his paw up in a little scrap of bandage to support it while it healed.

"Any other concerns," she said, "while you're here?"

Betsy knew that vets didn't do grandads, so she shook her head.

By the time she finally left the rain had stopped, and it was dark. She splashed through puddles and neatly dodged the spray thrown up by passing cars. Then she reached the common, and paused.

There was a sign at the edge of the grass:

FRY *and* SONS'
CIRCUS OF WONDERS

The finest circus acts in all the world

and

A very special GUEST ACT performing in London for the VERY FIRST TIME!

Don't miss this especially spectacular spectacle!

The circus tent was up. The roof had been hemmed with lights, and colourful streamers flew from the top. Giddy hurdy-gurdy music was playing, and people were crowding into the big top, leaving the damp London night for the warm light inside.

At the edge of the common, near where Betsy stood, tickets were being sold from a booth. A sign in front announced:

TICKETS JUST £5 EACH!

Betsy knew she had exactly five pounds in her pocket: it was her birthday money. She also knew she should walk straight home. But that longing was back again. And this was probably the only chance she would ever have to see her grandma's circus.

Her family wouldn't be home for a while yet. If she watched the show, they would never find out. And if nobody found out, then nobody would be hurt. So *that* was all right. Probably.

Betsy stepped on to the common and walked towards the booth. The mud was squishy underfoot and she lost her footing, almost slipping over. She righted herself, then hesitated.

"Roll up, roll up!" called the man at the booth. He wore a red jacket and a black top hat, and had an enormous voice. "A ticket for you, young lady? Quickly – we're starting any minute!"

Betsy could have sworn that she was opening her mouth to say, "No thank you." But somehow the words that came out were, "Yes please."

"Five pounds then, and step inside!"

Betsy reached into her pocket and paid her five pounds. Then she and her forty-four mice followed the footsteps of the grandma she had never met, out of the cold, into the sparkling world of Fry and Sons' Circus of Wonders.

OUR SECOND ACT

The Impossibly Hungry Mice

Inside the tent, it was crowded. Betsy and her mice were pushed this way and that as people made a beeline for the best seats. A particularly pushy push made her drop the case of mice, and she had to sink to her knees and rescue it from the sea of feet, which kept kicking it just out of reach. When it got wedged against a tent pole, she dived and grabbed it.

"Everyone OK?" she whispered, straightening up again. The mice seemed perfectly happy, in spite of their ordeal, although the case looked a little battered.

Wooden benches ran round the stage in raked circles. Betsy had only just found a space and squeezed in, tucking the mice under the seat, when the lights began to dim. A moment later the whole place was in darkness. The crowd hushed and murmured and shushed each other until they were silent. Everyone held their breath.

A single violin began to play. The audience watched the darkness, and waited.

Suddenly six flames appeared and began wheeling and turning through the dark. The crowd oohed in delight, and when the lights came up at last to reveal the fire juggler, they applauded and whistled and cheered. Betsy was applauding loudest of all.

The moment the lights were up, the rest of the performers joined the fire juggler onstage to parade round the ring. There were acrobats in sequins, clowns in bright silks, jugglers and strongmen and a magician, and a horse with bells and ribbons, and people twirling hula hoops. High above them, a tightrope walker waved from her rope. The violin was joined by an accordion and a drum, and the music they

played was so joyful that Betsy found her own feet dancing under the bench.

Then the ringmaster appeared in his red jacket and top hat: Mr Fry himself. It was the man who had sold Betsy her ticket. He was a small man, but his top hat was mighty and so was his voice. He threw out his arms and roared: "Ladies and gentlemen, welcome *tooooo* ... FRY AND SONS' CIRCUS OF WONDERS!"

And at this cue, everybody danced offstage, leaving the ringmaster to introduce the first act.

Betsy was spellbound. She had never known anything like it. As she watched people cartwheel and climb and spin and flip and swing through the air, she felt as though something inside her was flying with them, free and happy.

The show slipped by much too fast – a blur of silks and sparkles and smiles.

"That was the Fearless Flying Fernando, ladies and gentlemen!" cried Mr Fry, as the fearless Fernando flew fearlessly offstage and the crowd clapped excitedly. Stagehands quickly brought in a table covered in sequinned cloth while the ringmaster continued: "Now, we have just two more acts for you tonight, so please give them a warm welcome... Put your hands together for the most marvellous of magicians, the cleverest of conjurors ... ENOCH THE SPLENDID!"

The crowd cheered as a magician with an extravagant beard pranced onstage, beaming. He made all sorts of unlikely objects appear and disappear with cries of "Abracadabra!", ending with the traditional rabbit from a hat. He was so delighted by everything he did that you couldn't help smiling with him. Even the rabbit looked like it would laugh in surprise if it could – until it was duly made to disappear again.

Betsy had no idea when the problems began. She was still laughing and smiling with the magician as he exited the ring, and the jugglers and clowns appeared to entertain the crowd while the stage was prepared for the last act. And as the clowns chased each other with their custard pies, she was still blissfully unaware of the trouble to come.

But then the rabbit un-vanished itself from a hidden compartment in the magician's table. It no longer looked like it would laugh if it could. This was, unmistakably, a very annoyed rabbit.

A few people spotted it and they gasped and pointed, thinking it was all part of the act. Only Betsy noticed a couple of the tiny reddish-brown creatures that had disturbed it. Stomach turning, she bent down to check the case under her seat. F-to-F-sharp-first-octave was all alone.

"How...?" breathed Betsy. Then she noticed the latch. It must have been knocked in all the pushing and shoving before the show, and the door had been nosed ajar.

Betsy stared at the stage in horror. More mice were scurrying in and out of the rabbit's now-open compartment, which had food inside to keep the rabbit happy. Forty-four hungry noses must have sniffed it out, and forty-three hungry mice had followed the scent. The rabbit had left its hiding place and lolloped off across the ring in high dudgeon.

"Ohnoohn*o*," breathed Betsy. Should she

shout out, "Home!" and get them back? But before she could pluck up the courage to do this, stagehands were carrying the table offstage, and the mice were gone with it.

And maybe that would have been that if a juggler hadn't tripped over the rabbit. He bumped into two more jugglers as he fell. All three of them toppled to the ground, dropping balls and skittles everywhere.

At the sound of this commotion, the clowns paused. They had been merrily preparing to custard-pie each other in the face, but spotting the problem, they gave chase to the rabbit instead, pretending this was all meant to happen. They caught him as the music dropped to a tense hum, and everyone exited the stage just in time. A moment later, the lights went down and a spotlight lit up an acrobat suspended in mid-air by two silk ribbons. She waved gracefully to the crowd as the ringmaster came on to announce her.

"Ladies and gentlemen!" he roared. "We promised you a spectacular guest, here for her very first London performance. The time has come! I am *very* proud to present our grand finale – the wonder you've been waiting for – Seraphina of the Silks!"

Then two things happened at once.

First, there was a distinct, "*Bother*," and a lot of thumping. The rabbit had wriggled out of the clown's arms and run back into the ring. The clowns were giving chase, but they were hampered by the darkness, their custard pies and their massive shoes. It didn't sound like it was going well.

Second, Seraphina began a death-defying

tumble down her ribbons, spinning all the way to the bottom, only to catch herself an inch above the ground.

The spotlight followed her down. Just as she reached the bottom, one clown stumbled backwards, and tripped over a skittle. He waved his arms in a futile attempt to keep his balance, and pied Seraphina of the Silks in the face.

The crowd erupted into laughter and applause.

It was hard to be sure through all the custard, but Betsy didn't think that Seraphina of the Silks was laughing. With grave dignity, she stood up, shook off her ribbons, glared at the clown and walked out of the ring, leaving a trail of custard in her wake.

The crowd waited to see what would happen next.

The clown gave an awkward little bow. The silence went on slightly too long. The clown backed away through the curtains, and the rabbit lolloped off after him. The spotlight hung around awkwardly.

And then the ringmaster was back, smiling as though everything had gone perfectly, and calling on all the performers for their finale.

The music changed to a jig and the crowd clapped in time, but they were all murmuring to each other: *Was that meant to happen? Did you see the rabbit? Did you see the look on Seraphina's face?*

When the lights came up, the murmuring swelled excitedly and everyone left the tent, gossiping loudly. Betsy sat alone as the chattering crowd swarmed past her, clutching the empty case. She felt hot with shame for the trouble she had caused. Now she was going to have to go and ask for her mice back, and apologize. The thought made her heart hammer.

But there was no time to lose – she had to get home before her family did, because the idea of telling them where she had been made her heart hammer in her throat as well.

When the last person had left, Betsy made herself get up. She descended the raked benches, crossed the stage and pushed through two sets of curtains at the back, out to the world behind the big top.

Around her was a semicircle of trailers. They had brightly lit windows with checked curtains, and doors painted with beautiful pictures. These were the performers' homes.

Betsy tried not to panic. She just had to work out which of the trailers the magician lived in, and ask for her mice back. Quickly.

She hurried to the nearest trailer and began peering through windows. Luck was on her side: at the third trailer, she could see the greatly bearded silhouette of Enoch the Splendid. It looked like a friendly sort of silhouette. The kind that might say, "Never mind, no harm done, have your mice back and hurry home." Probably. It's hard to tell with silhouettes. There was only one way to find out.

Betsy took a deep breath, and knocked.

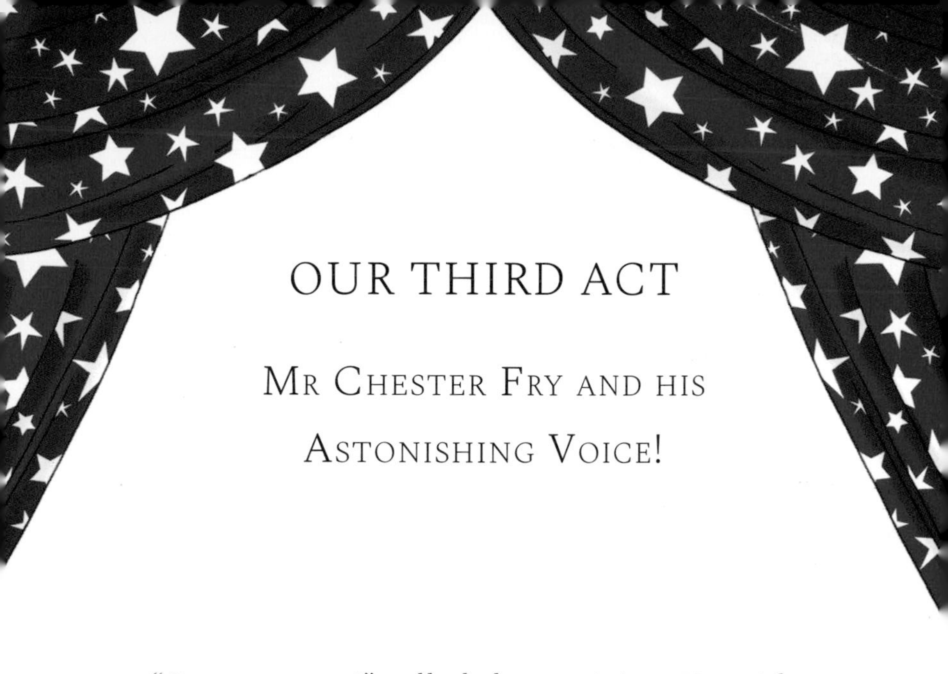

OUR THIRD ACT

Mr Chester Fry and his Astonishing Voice!

"Open sesame!" called the magician. He said it as though the very idea of opening a door tickled and delighted him.

So Betsy open sesame-d, and coughed. "Um. Excuse me."

Enoch the Splendid turned to face her. Up close, Betsy could see that he was very elderly and that his beard was even more massive and luxurious than it had appeared onstage, pouring in thick curls down to his knees.

Above the beard, two bright eyes twinkled.

He twiddled a curl of beard in confused delight. "A mysterious visitor!"

"Hello, Mr – ah – Enoch the Splendid." Betsy wasn't sure if this was the right way to address him, but it seemed rude just to say Enoch.

"Please," said Enoch the Splendid. "My friends all call me the Splendid."

"Oh. Hello, er – the Splendid," said Betsy. "Um. My name's Betsy. I'm sorry to interrupt. It's just that, you see, my mice are in your table." Now she said it out loud, this didn't sound as reasonable as she had hoped.

"I'm afraid I don't see that at *all*," said the Splendid. "But it sounds tremendously interesting. Tell me again. Your *what* are in *which*?"

"My mice," said Betsy. And she told him everything that had happened. She had been afraid he would be cross, but he was much too busy chuckling and twiddling his beard. She liked him at once.

"Well, well," he said, "what a to-do. Come in then, Betsy, and collect your runaway mice. Well, *well.*" And he gestured, with the sweep of a velvet-clad arm, that she should step into his trailer. "If I were you," he confided, shutting the door, "I'd keep this little story between us. Mr Fry might not see the funny side. Now let's find those mice."

If Betsy hadn't been in such a hurry, she would have enjoyed looking round the Splendid's trailer. It was a tiny house with a kitchenette in one corner and a bed in the other. And it was crammed from floor to ceiling with every object you could think of – flowers and eggs and coins and marbles and a pocket watch and saws and scarves and fans and mirrors and playing cards and a bag of hay for the rabbit...

But there was no time to admire it all. She hurried to the magic table, opened the case and called the mice home. They all came at a trot. F-to-F-sharp squeaked for joy to see them.

"What beautiful creatures!" the Splendid exclaimed. "Where—"

But before he could finish the question there was a knock at the door, and a voice roared, "ENOCH!"

"Alas," he whispered, "it sounds as though Mr Fry is in quite a temper. I would not recommend meeting him. Would you care to wait in this vanishing cabinet a moment? I assure you it won't *really* vanish you."

Betsy checked her watch uncertainly. But then the ringmaster pounded on the door again, and the pounding was so fierce that she found her feet had taken her inside the vanishing cabinet before her brain had made a decision either way. It was a good hiding place, and it would have had plenty of room for Betsy and her mice except that the Splendid was also using it to store a life-size model ostrich.

While Betsy worked out how to arrange

herself so that she wasn't being poked by a large beak, she heard the Splendid open the trailer door. "Chester," he said. "To what do I owe the pleasure?"

"What took you so long?" Betsy couldn't see the ringmaster, but she could hear him loud and clear. "Now listen, Enoch. I made it very clear that we could only have that rabbit if you *absolutely promised me* it would behave itself."

"Indeed, I recall. If I may—"

"Seraphina has walked out," said Fry. "Surprisingly, she can't see the funny side of a custard pie in the face. Her enormous ego must be blocking the view."

"Goodness me. Perhaps—"

"Tomorrow, Enoch, three very rich people are coming to see the show. If they're impressed, they will invest money in our tour.

They're not easy to impress: I only persuaded them to come at all by promising a spectacular closing act. Now I don't have one."

"Ah," said the Splendid.

"Can you pull a new act out of a hat for me, Enoch? Something London has never seen?"

"My dear Chester, I don't believe any of my hats are large enough."

Chester Fry pounded something and there was a crash from the shelves. The ostrich wobbled, and tumbled into Betsy, poking feathers into her ears and eyes and nose. She tried very hard not to sneeze.

"This is no time for jokes. You're fired. Take your rabbit and get out."

There was a pause. In the vanishing cabinet, Betsy wished it *could* make her vanish after all. Before, she had just felt embarrassed. Now it turned out that her mice had caused some really serious trouble.

"But Chester—" began the Splendid.

"Don't *but Chester* me!" roared Fry. "You promised me that creature would never leave its hiding place. That was a lie. It's ruined the show!"

Betsy waited for the Splendid to explain that it wasn't really his rabbit's fault at all, but forty-four entirely unexpected mice. She braced herself to meet Chester Fry and confess. But the Splendid didn't say anything of the sort. He just said, "Well, well."

He was protecting her. But why? He didn't even know her. Betsy couldn't allow it. She was going to have to be the one to tell the truth then.

She decided this very firmly, but what her head decided and her body did were two very different things. It was like trying to get out of bed. She counted down from three. Then she counted again, really meaning it this time. Then she heard the magician say, "Well, *well*," a second time, even more sadly; so she took a deep breath and opened the vanishing cabinet door.

The ostrich tumbled out, and pecked Chester Fry smartly on the head as it fell.

"Oh," said Betsy. "*Sorry.*"

"Ah. Um – abracadabra?" suggested the Splendid.

Fry didn't know whether he should be directing his fury at the Splendid or Betsy or the ostrich; so he just pounded a chair in general rage and roared, "WHAT IS GOING ON?"

So Betsy told him, as best she could. The Splendid kept trying to interrupt, so she had to talk fast to stop him taking the blame. She couldn't quite meet Fry's eyes. He had looked much more friendly with his top hat on: without it, you could see his enormous frown, which seemed to be a permanent feature of his face.

"So it was my mice that started it all, not the rabbit," she concluded. "Please don't fire Mr Splendid." And she risked looking Fry in the eyes. The fury she saw made her face burn.

"It's a bit late for *please*, girl," he boomed. He was a small man, but his great voice seemed to tower over all of them, even the Splendid. "If I don't get those investors on board, I'm going to have to fire a lot of people, not just Enoch. This circus badly needs that money."

"Oh," said Betsy. So her confession hadn't put things right. She looked at her feet. "Sorry," she said again – which wasn't enough, but she couldn't think of anything else to say.

And then she did think of something else to say – something that could put things right – and her heart did a skittery sort of wibble.

"What if," she said, and then her heart wibbled again and she had to restart. "What if I could find another act to impress your investors?"

Fry and the Splendid looked at her.

"The thing is, my mice—" began Betsy, and then she decided it might be easier just to show them. So she put the carry case on top of the table, and opened the door. "Line up, please," she said. "F-to-F-sharp-first-octave, you stay."

The injured mouse curled up sadly in his cubbyhole as the other forty-three mice filed out in a line, and eighty-six eyes looked alertly at Betsy. They were so smart and neat about it that the Splendid gave a little, "Oh", of admiration, and even Fry leaned forwards to see what would happen next.

"OK. Cartwheel."

Forty-three tiny mice took to their front paws in unison, and wheeled joyfully. Two human men blinked and rubbed their eyes.

"Tower," said Betsy, and the mice began to assemble into a great mouse-column.

"Forward roll."

"Star jumps."

"Mr Splendid, do you have any string? Thank you." She held the string out in a taut line. "Mice: tightrope. Now on your back paws. Now on your front paws."

And so the show went on. Betsy was so absorbed in the tiny spins and flips of the mice that for a minute she forgot all about Fry and the Splendid. But when the last mouse had performed its final pirouette and she had sent them scampering to their case, she looked up.

"That's it really," she said. "I could try and teach them some other things..."

The Splendid broke out into enthusiastic applause. Fry did not applaud, but his frown looked a bit less furious and a bit more thoughtful. When the Splendid's applause had died awkwardly away, he nodded. "Enoch," he said, "I will need five hundred pairs of binoculars by tomorrow night. Find them for me. And you," he said to Betsy, "will be here at four o'clock sharp with those mice."

It was suddenly all very real. Betsy thought

of Grandad, and hesitated. But Fry saw the hesitation and added, "Of course, maybe you're busy. In which case, we'll just have to tell the investors that there is no finale and I will have to begin cutting costs. Enoch, you'd better start packing..."

And that was that. Betsy couldn't let the innocent magician lose his job over something that she had started. So she said, "I'll be there."

Fry put his hands on his hips. "With a proper costume, mind – something impressive."

Betsy had no idea how she would manage that. But she nodded.

"Good," boomed Fry. "What's your name?"

"Betsy," said Betsy.

"I will see you tomorrow, Betsy. Four o'clock. Don't be late." And with one last frown at the Splendid, and another at the ostrich for good measure, Fry stormed from the trailer, slamming the door behind him.

The Splendid smiled and his beard fanned out enormously. "Well, well, *well*," he said, "what miraculous mice! Are you sure you don't mind being in our little show?"

"I don't mind," said Betsy. She couldn't work out whether this was a lie. On the one hand, she felt very guilty. On the other hand, she felt a bit dizzy with excitement. And this, of course, only made her feel more guilty.

"Well, thank you, little Miss Sprightly."

Betsy opened her mouth to reply, then realized what he had said and stared at him.

He chuckled. "Oh, I guessed as soon as I saw you; then when you told me about the mice I was entirely certain. You're the spitting image of your grandmother, Betsy. And she was my best friend, once upon a time – in fact, she used to appear from that very vanishing cabinet at the end of my act, to start her own performance."

"Oh!" said Betsy, not sure what to say to this. She wasn't used to people speaking so warmly and openly about Grandma. No wonder, then, that the magician had been so kind to her. But his kindness only made Betsy feel worse. And she didn't *want* to be the spitting image of Grandma. She belonged to Grandad.

While Fry was there, she had forgotten all about Grandad and home. Now she realized with horror that she had no idea how much time had passed. Her stomach turned. "Mr Splendid," she said, grabbing the case. "I have to go right now. Sorry. I have to get home before my family do."

"Your family aren't here?"

"No," said Betsy. "They ... er ... they don't really..."

The Splendid smiled sadly. "You don't have to explain. I can imagine the rest. Off you run then, my dear. I'll see you tomorrow." And he held open the door for her with a flourish.

Betsy said goodbye and hurried out of the trailer. The rain had begun again, and the brightly lit trailers looked cosy; you could hear talk and laughter coming from inside them, snug and content. Betsy felt that same longing.

But there was no time to think about that. Her family could be back any minute – for all she knew, they were there already. With the mice tucked under one arm, Betsy put the Circus of Wonders out of her mind and raced across the common – back to her home.

OUR FOURTH ACT

Grandma's Star-spangled Cloak!

As Betsy neared the edge of the common, she saw the silhouettes of Grandad and Bella walking down the road. They were a minute from the house still, but she wouldn't get to the front door without them seeing. She had taken too long.

There was no time to lose. She broke into a run and went down a side street at double speed. Then she tore down the alley behind the gardens of her road, slipped through the old gap in the fence and raced over to the kitchen window.

She had learned as a small girl how to lever this open from the outside so she could slither into the kitchen. It occurred to her halfway through that she was not as small any more, but it was too late for that now; she shoved and pushed and wriggled, and at last landed in the kitchen sink. She shut the window, put the mice down on the counter and pulled herself round into a sitting position, feet dangling.

But before she could drop to the floor, Bella opened the kitchen door with Grandad behind her.

"Hello, darling!" said Bella. "Um. What are you doing in the sink?"

Betsy tried to look like someone who is in a sink on purpose. "Playing."

"What's the game?"

She couldn't think of any good games involving sinks. She looked at the draining board for inspiration, and heard herself say, "Washing-up. I'm … pretending to be a spoon."

Luckily, Bella was used to her daughter having strange ideas. She just laughed and kissed her forehead. But when she had gone to hang up her coat, Grandad raised his eyebrows at Betsy.

Betsy did her best impression of an innocent spoon, but she felt terrible.

"B," said Grandad. "Do spoons normally wear coats and shoes?"

Betsy was saved from answering this by the arrival of Bertram. "Hello! What's going on here then?"

"Playing washing-up," said Betsy miserably.

"She's a spoon," explained Grandad, giving Betsy a Look.

"Aha." Bertram thought about this, then got up on the draining board and did his earnest best to be spoon-like. He got quite into it.

Betsy was stuck playing washing-up for another half an hour while her father experimented with being a salad bowl, a bread knife and a cheese grater. But at least it saved her from Grandad's questions, and her own thoughts.

When washing-up was over and dinner had been eaten she went hastily to bed, which warded off the questions again, but then she couldn't avoid thinking. She lay awake, going over everything for hours, until long after everyone else had gone to bed. But however many times she went over it, it was hard to really believe she would be performing in the circus tomorrow. It had all happened so fast.

Betsy hated keeping secrets, and she felt terrible about Grandad. But she had a debt to pay the Splendid and the circus, and that was that. She just had to roll up her sleeves and set about putting things right. She tried to focus on the important questions – like how to get away tomorrow and where to find a costume – and not to think too hard about Grandad with his raised eyebrows and his sad-worm-elbows.

Next to her the mice chittered and chirruped in their sleep, blissfully unaware that they were soon to be circus stars. Betsy loved them, but they weren't much use when it came to conversation and right now that made her feel more alone than ever. She wondered if Grandma had ever felt that way. Had she missed having Grandad to talk to?

With that thought, Betsy suddenly knew

exactly where to find a costume.

It was risky. But she didn't have any other ideas – and if she was going to do it, she had to act now, while everyone else was asleep. She got up and padded very quietly to the door.

The Bow-Linnets' house was full of creaks and groans and surprising thuds. Also, Betsy had forgotten about the Christmas decorations and set off a herd of bells that had been wrapped around the banister.

"*Shhhhh*," she said.

Tinktinktinktink, replied the bells.

Betsy stood very still, waiting for the sound of someone getting out of bed. Nothing came. She tiptoed across the landing, opened the door to Grandad's study and slipped inside.

With the door shut behind her, the room was utterly dark, apart from the very last embers in the fireplace. They winked at her encouragingly.

The trouble with finding anything in Grandad's study in the dark was that you never knew when you might be ambushed by an unexpected pile of Stuff. Most rooms in the house were well behaved and Stuff stayed roughly where you expected it to be. Grandad's Stuff moved around and seemed to somehow multiply, so that you never quite knew *what* you would find.

Eventually, once she had made it past a pile of books and an entirely unexpected and very large globe, Betsy reached the desk. She opened the large drawer on the bottom left-hand side. Last summer, she had discovered that this was Grandad's Drawer of Grandma.

She carefully lifted out the pile of papers, which she knew were all the newspaper articles and photos that Grandad had kept. Underneath, just as she had remembered, there was a large box. She took it out, and put the papers back.

Only now did what she was doing really hit her. The study had the musty, comfortable smell of Grandad, and it was so overwhelming that Betsy had a sudden urge to run and hug him and tell him everything and say that she was sorry. But she didn't, for two reasons.

First, he was asleep, and only fools disturbed Grandad when he was asleep; and second, it would only make him more unhappy. It would be a selfish thing to do.

Betsy opened the box and felt inside. Her hand met crushed velvet, cool and soft; her grandma's cloak. She pulled it out and put it on. It settled heavily around her shoulders. It was much too big, of course, but it would just have to trail behind her magnificently. She swayed very slightly, making the ends swirl, and found herself wondering what her grandma had been like.

The thought felt dangerous. She took the cloak off and folded it carefully into its box.

By now, the last ember had winked and died, and the darkness felt very lonely. Betsy groped across the desk, found a lamp and turned it on. Then she sat on the floor and leafed through the pile of papers. Her grandma smiled out at her from newspaper cuttings, sometimes young, sometimes old. There were loose photos of her with Grandad, and sometimes a baby Bella. Grandma had Betsy's curls and a gap-toothed smile. Betsy *almost* thought she looked nice.

There were envelopes addressed to Grandad in jaunty, curly handwriting that Betsy didn't open. They felt private. But one letter in the pile didn't have an envelope and it had different handwriting – slanted, tall letters in indigo ink. Betsy picked it up.

Mr Bow,

I will tell you plainly, sir, that your letter is a waste of time. I cannot and will not do as you ask.

You speak of betrayal. There has been no betrayal. The only disloyalty in this whole sorry story is Beryl's decision to abandon our circus in the first place.

Your feelings on the matter do not concern me. To be frank, I was surprised to receive your letter. Beryl is no longer any concern of yours.

C. Fry

Betsy stared at the letter. Poor Grandad. He must have written to Fry when Grandma left him. And this was all he had been given by way of reply. Betsy hadn't liked Fry, but now she loathed him.

And she, Betsy, was going to perform in his circus – just like her grandma before her. How could she have almost thought Grandma looked nice? Nobody nice could leave Grandad behind to go and work for a man like Mr Fry.

The Splendid's voice came back to her: *You're the spitting image of your grandmother, Betsy.* Betsy clenched her fists. She didn't want it to be true. She wished she could undo the whole evening and start again.

But it was no good wishing. She had to leave the Grandadish smell quickly, before her resolve wavered and she ran to wake him after all. Hastily, she put the lid on the cloak's box – in the lamplight she saw it was a deep blue and covered in sequinned stars – turned out the lamp and hurried back to her room. She shoved the cloak under her bed and lay there, staring up at the ceiling.

She tried counting sheep. She tried pretending to be a spoon. She didn't sleep for a long time.

When she did sleep at last, she dreamed muddled and confusing dreams where she was in a travelling circus show, with a cloak that spread out across the night sky, and she travelled from star to star on a tightrope, and it was wonderful. But it was terrible too, because she could see her home a long way below and however hard she tried, she couldn't find her way back.

OUR FIFTH ACT

The World's Smallest Acrobats!

It was surprisingly easy to arrange to get away the next day. In the morning, Betsy said she had been invited to her friend Molly's, because Molly lived at the end of the road and Betsy would be allowed to walk herself there. Actually, Molly was on holiday, but Betsy's parents didn't know that.

Then there was nothing to do but wait. She tried to settle to a book in the parlour, but all the guilt from last night was still there, heavy and sort of lumpy in her chest. She kept forgetting to read, and stared off into the distance instead, picking at threads in her old armchair. For a while, Grandad came in to water the ferns and Betsy tried to concentrate, but hearing him pottering about made her feel even worse.

When it was time to go, she packed the cloak into her rucksack and the mice into their travelling case.

"I'm going to take the mice to show Molly," she told Bella.

Bella was sorting through music at the kitchen table. She looked up, but her eyes were still full of dancing crotchets and quavers. "Good idea, darling. Have a wonderful time."

"Bye, Dad," said Betsy, poking her head

round the parlour door.

"Bye, Molly, have fun with Betsy," said Bertram, who was concentrating on his crossword.

Grandad came down the stairs. "You're off?"

"Yes."

"Have fun. And B?"

"Yes?"

"Whatever it is that you're keeping to yourself, it doesn't look fun. You know that you can always talk to me about anything, don't you?"

Betsy didn't trust herself to speak. She just nodded.

"If I ever catch you pretending to be cutlery again," he said, "we're going to have to have a serious talk." And he gave her a hug. Then he kept hugging her. Very hard. For a long time.

Betsy pulled herself free to look at him.

"Grandad," she said. "Are *you* feeling any be—"

"You're going to be late, B!" said Grandad. "Time to skedaddle!"

So he *wasn't* feeling better then. Betsy couldn't look at him as she left. Once the door was safely shut behind her, she ran all the way to the circus, as though she could blow everything out of her mind if she ran fast enough.

There was a tearing wind that day and when Betsy arrived, the streamers were fluttering furiously from the big top. But as she stepped inside the tent, the wind and the world outside dropped away. All that remained was Fry and Sons' Circus of Wonders.

The Wonders themselves were all in the ring, stretching or practising their acts or milling about and talking. Stagehands checked ropes and lights and went back and forth with props. Betsy had been so busy feeling guilty that she had forgotten to feel nervous, but now she felt *very* nervous, and unusually shy, seeing all these Wonders talking and laughing together as though they were just ordinary people.

The Splendid spotted her and waved. "Betsy!

Welcome! Come along – come and meet the family!" So Betsy did, and they were all so friendly and kind that she soon forgot about being shy. Everyone was very excited to say hello to the mice, and pleased to have her in the show.

The strongwoman clapped Betsy on the shoulder, which nearly toppled her over. "Nervous, little one?"

"Yes," said Betsy, "a bit."

"Don't be!" said one of the clowns as he laced up his enormous shoes. "You don't ever need to be nervous in the circus. Whatever happens in the ring, everybody else has got your back. We're a family." And there were murmurs of agreement from all sides, and even from above, which was confusing. Betsy looked up to see the tightrope walker smiling down at her.

They were all so welcoming that Betsy couldn't help wondering... "Mr Splendid," she whispered, when she could get a moment alone with him. "Did all these people know my grandma?"

"Oh no," he said. "She moved on from this circus years and years ago. There aren't many of us left from her time now – apart from Chester, of course."

Betsy hadn't thought of that. "Do you think he's realized I'm her granddaughter?"

"I'm not sure..."

As though he had been summoned, Chester Fry appeared at the edge of the ring. Betsy heard him before she saw him. "Betsy!" he bellowed. "There you are. Well, get practising – come along. We haven't got all day." He looked around at the rest of his Wonders.

"Why are half of you not in costume? Is this a circus or a party? Everybody get to work!" And he stood with his hands on his hips, waiting.

The chatter died away. Fry seemed to have drained all the colour and sparkle from the Wonders, who went about their work without a word. But Fry wasn't watching them: his frown was focused on Betsy. When she let the mice out on the Splendid's table to begin a run-through, his eyes followed their every move. It didn't bother them at all, but it made Betsy more nervous than ever. She put on the cloak for courage.

The mice behaved perfectly, but all Fry had to say was, "Good. Make sure they don't run off," before he went out to greet the crowd and sell tickets. With him gone, Betsy could breathe again; but then a stagehand gave the signal to clear the ring so that the audience could be let inside. Betsy summoned the mice home, and her hand was trembling as she did up the latch. The Splendid and the strongwoman appeared on either side of her and they all walked back to the trailers, Betsy clutching the case.

"All well, my dear?" asked the Splendid.

"I think so, thanks," said Betsy.

"Are your family coming to see the show?" asked the strongwoman.

"Um, no," said Betsy, "They're ... busy." The Splendid looked at her with sad understanding and changed the subject.

"Those mice, Betsy! How *do* you train them? And tell me, do you have to use a special comb to keep their whiskers so perky?"

So Betsy told the Splendid stories about

the mice, which helped take her mind off her fluttering stomach a bit. Then they sat on the steps of his trailer, eating popcorn for dinner and watching everyone rush to and fro. They heard the reports of the crowd from the stagehands: a full house, they said. Excited, they said. There were three very snooty VIPs in ringside seats, they said, who had all been given free candyfloss and were getting it all over their fine clothes.

Betsy concentrated on that last bit. This wasn't about what she wanted, or what her family wanted. It wasn't even about that big, excited crowd, although thinking about them did strange things to her tummy. It was only about those candyfloss-covered investors and the money they could bring in to save the circus. It was about the debt she owed the Splendid, and everybody else who called Fry's Circus their home.

"Ready?" she whispered to the box of mice on her lap.

The mice were all very busy cleaning their paws and playing with their tails and so on. One looked suspiciously like it was pretending to be a spoon. Anyway, they didn't answer her.

"Of course you're ready," said Betsy. "So am I. I think."

Then the call came for the opening number. The fire dancer stepped inside the tent, ready to go and twirl his flames in the darkness.

It was strange to see how the show looked from backstage. Betsy and the Splendid sat on the trailer steps for the whole thing, their breath misting in the cold night air, Betsy wrapped in her grandma's warm cloak. They watched as people disappeared into the big top, then burst back out again, hurrying off for a costume change or jogging on the spot to keep warm while they waited to run back in. Then a stagehand came to call the last two acts: the Splendid, and Betsy.

"Good luck, Betsy!" whispered the Splendid. And she whispered good luck back, once to him and once to the mice as she handed them over. The mice went onstage with him on top of his table, to wait for her there. Betsy was left alone in the wings.

In no time at all, people were cheering the Splendid and Fry was instructing the audience to ready their binoculars. For a moment, nerves threatened to overwhelm Betsy. Then Fry called her name and there was no time to be nervous. There was only time to get on with the show.

She strode out into the ring, arms aloft, and discovered three things at once.

First, stage lights work two ways. They light up the performers for the audience, but they also hide the audience from the performers. Beyond the dazzling ring, Betsy couldn't see a thing.

Second, there is a special sound to hundreds of unseen people watching you.

It's a bit like silence, but it feels as though somebody has pulled that silence tight, and it's full of tiny shuffles and coughs.

Third, stage lights are hot. Very hot. The kind of hot that means a heavy velvet cloak is really not ideal.

But this was not the time to fuss about that. The invisible audience was expecting her. So Betsy marched forwards to where her mice waited on the table; then she opened the case.

"Line up!" she declared, in a great theatrical voice, which took her entirely by surprise. And forty-three of her wonderful, beautiful mice lined up, eyes twinkling, whiskers aflutter, without a care in the world. Watching them, all fear left Betsy.

"Handstand!" she announced.

The mice flipped on to their front paws.

From the darkness there came the *shwup* of hundreds of people giving a sharp intake of breath at the same time.

"Cartwheel! Star jumps! Mexican wave!"

They were off. The audience was in the palm of Betsy's hand – and of one hundred

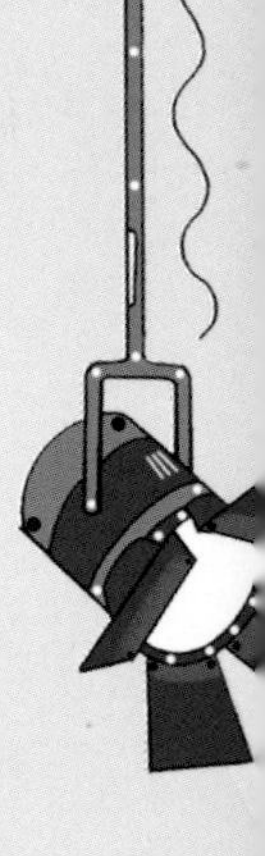

and seventy-two tiny paws, of course. Every trick drew gasps and applause.

"Tightrope! Back paws! Front paws!"

It was easy. It was wonderful. It was like discovering that you knew how to fly.

"Forward roll! Through the hoop! Pirouette!"

It was all Betsy wanted to do, ever. It felt *right*.

"Bow!"

It was over much too fast. Betsy felt as if she'd only just stepped onstage, but now the mice were bowing, and she was bowing, and the invisible audience was going absolutely berserk. They kept going berserk for ages and ages. Betsy had to bow twice – three times – four times. Then at last Fry came trotting onstage, shouting, "Ladies and gentlemen, the world's tiniest acrobats!"

That was Betsy's cue to leave. So just like that, she called the mice home, bowed once more, waved and departed in a swirl of velvet, the cheering still ringing in her ears.

The others were all clustered in the wings, ready for the finale. There was a flutter of warmly whispered *well dones* from all sides, and *that* was better than all the applause in the world.

"Sounds like they loved you!" said the strongwoman, giving Betsy a mildly terrifying squeeze on the shoulder.

A beard tickled her elbow as the Splendid whispered, "Of course they did!"

"Great job, little one!"

"Marvellous, Betsy!"

Then they were all dancing into the ring and Betsy was alone in the darkness. She tried hard to hold on to the feeling of it all, so that she could keep it safe inside her memory. But she knew it was already slipping away.

OUR SIXTH ACT

THE STAGGERING TREACHERY OF CHESTER FRY!

It was over. The crowd had left in a chattering swarm and the stagehands were clearing the stage, carrying things to and fro and talking about what to have for dinner. It was time for Betsy to get back to her family.

She looked at everything with doubly fierce concentration, to make sure she remembered it all. The flag fluttered like *that.* The lights twinkled like *that.* The mingled smell of popcorn and dry ice and hundreds of people all closely packed together still clung to her cloak, and it was like *that.*

Then she turned her back on it all, thought of home and made herself walk away.

But she had only gone three paces when a hand fell on her shoulder. She looked round to see Chester Fry, who was having a go at smiling. He still had the usual frown, so overall it looked as though his face had been uncomfortably squashed at both ends.

"Come along, Betsy," he said. "The investors want to shake your hand."

It wasn't a request: Betsy was already being steered by the shoulder, away from the other trailers, round to Fry's. It was set a little way apart, slightly larger than the others, next to a sleek red car with FRY on the number plate. She didn't mind meeting the investors, if it would help, but she wished Fry would let go of her shoulder.

Inside, three women in smart evening dresses were standing, holding glasses of champagne. They were ecstatic to meet Betsy and to see the mice up close.

"So sweet!" cried one.

"So clever!" cried another.

"Whiskers, yes, good," mumbled the third, who seemed to be having a lot more champagne than anybody else.

Betsy took out a mouse for everyone to meet and he behaved perfectly, spinning and bowing on cue. They were all thrilled, and Betsy began to worry that the cooing and admiring would never end. But at last the champagne was finished, the mouse was put away, and the investors were saying their goodbyes and shaking Betsy's hand.

They were ushered out and Betsy went to follow – but Fry's hand was on her shoulder once again.

"One moment, Betsy," he announced, shutting the door. "Sit," he said, pointing to a chair.

So Betsy sat. It was a soft, plump little chair, with shiny gold swirls on the arms.

Fry's trailer was full of shiny gold swirls and much plusher than the Splendid's. He sat in the armchair opposite, and put a footstool between them for Betsy to rest the case of mice on. She put them down and waited for him to explain, an uneasy feeling in her belly.

"I'll come straight to the point," he said. "We're moving on to the next town, and you can come with us. I'm offering you a place in my circus."

"Oh!" For a moment, Betsy had a wild image of her and the mice in their own trailer with checked curtains and a painted door, on the road with the rest of the Wonders. But she squashed it hastily. "Thank you, Mr Fry, but I can't."

"Why not? We can delay leaving until tomorrow, if you need time..."

Betsy almost asked where they were going, but she decided she didn't want to know. "I'm sorry – I'd love to – but I can't leave my family."

"I see." In one elastic movement, Fry dropped the smile and doubled his frown. "In that case, we have a problem. The investors are expecting you to come with us. They won't be giving us any money without your mice."

So Betsy hadn't repaid her debt, after all. That made her feel terrible. But there was no question of joining the circus. "I'm sorry about that," she said. "Truly. But I have to go." And she stood to leave, before she could change her mind.

The moment she stood, Fry's little hand shot out, and his fingers hooked on to the case of mice.

Betsy reached to stop him, but she was too slow. He opened the case and brought a mouse out on his finger. It had a bandage and moved on to his palm with a slight limp: F-to-F-sharp-first-octave.

"Beautiful little things," he remarked, holding the mouse up to his face. "Handstand!" he said. And hearing the command, F-to-F-sharp valiantly had a go with the weight on his good paw, his bad paw trembling on Fry's palm. "It would have been better to have you with us, Betsy; you could have taught them new tricks. But I took a note of the commands, so if you won't come, we'll just stick to the old ones. I'll do your act myself."

"Give them back!" said Betsy. "I'll yell! I'll yell for help!"

"I wouldn't do that," said Fry. "If I were you." Very gently, he stroked F-to-F-sharp.

"I'll call—" But then Betsy had to break off her threats to say, "You have to be careful with him. Don't hold him or you'll squash him."

"Yes," agreed Fry. "I imagine I would." His fingers closed round F-to-F-sharp in a loose circle, not quite touching him. "How many mice are there, Betsy? Forty? Forty-two?"

"Forty-four," said Betsy. "Please be careful. He—"

"Is that so?" said Fry. "I wonder how many people counted. I'm sure our investors didn't. Good thing, having so many – we could lose a few and the act wouldn't suffer at all." He flexed his fingers: Betsy briefly saw two frightened eyes, before the mouse was hidden again.

"Please," she said. "Please put him down."

"It's a shame," Fry went on, "that you won't be joining us. But since you say you *can't*, Betsy, you will leave this circus in sixty seconds. I will be watching you. You will talk to no one as you go."

"I—"

"Sixty," said Fry, looking at his watch. "Fifty-nine. Fifty-eight."

Betsy didn't move. She was trying to have a good idea. Or any idea at all.

"Fifty-seven. Fifty-six. Fifty-five." Fry's fingers tightened and F-to-F-sharp squeaked in alarm. Betsy got up hastily and tugged the trailer door open.

"Goodbye! Fifty-three. Fifty-two." The pitiful squeaking continued, and Betsy still had no ideas, so she stepped out into the cold. Fry walked to the door. "Remember," he said. "Talk to no one. Forty-nine. Forty-eight."

Tears stung Betsy's eyes, but she kept walking, and she talked to no one. She walked until she knew, logically, that she was too far away to hear a pygmy mouse squealing. But she still listened, and it seemed to her that she *could* hear it: a very faint plea that she could do nothing about except keep walking.

Fry watched until she was out of sight.

"Goodbye," he said. "Little Miss Sprightly."

OUR SEVENTH ACT

Betsy Bow Linnet's Perilous Mouse Rescue!

At home, Betsy hurried upstairs. The baubles tinkled and gossiped as she pushed past.

"Betsy?" called her mother. "Is that you?"

"Yup! Just putting the mice away!"

Tinktinktink, the baubles murmured in merry disapproval. Betsy shut the door on them and breathed deeply. She hated the lie and she hated keeping secrets, but what else could she do? How could she ever tell her mother what she had done?

Footsteps came tip-tapping up the stairs. Betsy hastily grabbed two ferns and put them in front of the mice's glass tank, hiding it from view. It would do for now, but it wouldn't work forever.

"Darling?" Bella curled her head round the door. "Did you have a nice time?"

"Mmm."

The rest of Bella curled itself in after her head. "You look a bit pale! Is everything OK?"

"Mmmm. I mean, no. I think I'm a bit ill. I might just go to bed."

This resulted in a lot of questions and feeling-of-forehead and hugs, which all made Betsy feel terrible; but it did at least distract her mother from the squeakless silence in the room. And it bought Betsy time alone, away from worried questions. After tucking her into her duvet, and feeling her forehead just one more time for luck, Bella turned out the light and left Betsy to her thoughts.

Betsy tried to work out what her thoughts *were*, but they were running amok and it was difficult. She had let the mice down, and when her family realized and asked where they had gone, they would find out that she had let *them* down, and it was all just an endless maze of letting-people-down whichever way she turned.

Five minutes later, Bertram poked his head round the door to see if Betsy's illness was the kind that got better if you had a quick bit of cake and milk. Betsy pretended to be asleep.

Ten minutes later, Grandad came in.

"Your father says you're asleep," he whispered, "but *I* say you're a cheeky pretender." Betsy opened her eyes and Grandad winked. "Oldest trick in the book, B. I pretended to nap for three days straight once when your mother wanted me to have a birthday party." He kissed her on the cheek. "Sweet pretend dreams. I won't give you away. But in the morning you and I are going to have a chat about whatever-it-is, all right?"

Then he left too, leaving Betsy feeling worse than ever.

But feeling bad wasn't helping anybody. If Betsy was going to roll up her sleeves and put things right, she needed to focus. The circus was leaving tomorrow. She would have to try and steal the mice back tonight.

First, she had to wait for the family to go to bed. It was a long wait. Grandad's shuffle came first. Then Bertram's slippers, then the tip-tap of Bella.

Betsy gave Bella five minutes. Then ten. Then fifteen just to make sure she was really asleep. By now, the thought of leaving her warm bed to hunt for the mice in the shadows of the common without any sort of plan was a lot less appealing. Wouldn't it make more sense, after all, to go over there in daylight when she could think straight? Had Fry said what time tomorrow they would leave?

And then Betsy remembered. He had only offered to leave the next day for her sake. They might leave tonight. *They might already have left.*

She was out of her bed and into the hall like an arrow, forgetting to bother about the creaky house, and running down the stairs to the bay window in the parlour. She pushed through the ferns, setting off every bauble, and looked out.

The tent had gone. Her heart skipped a beat. But then she made out the hulking shapes of trailers hitched up to cars. So the big top had been packed away, but they hadn't left yet.

Still, packing meant they really were going. There was no time to lose. Before she had time to think twice, she was fishing out the spare key from the sideboard, along with one of the many bags of pumpkin seeds. She sat down to do up her trainers, tugging at the laces fiercely and tying them tight, as though she was strapping on armour. Then she zipped up her coat over her pyjamas, put the key and pumpkin seeds in her pocket and opened the door.

She would be in *so* much trouble if she was caught sneaking out at night. But there wasn't time to worry about that.

The wreath flapped as she closed the door behind her. In her memory, Grandad sang, "Ding dong merrily on *hiiiigh,* a mouse has chewed this *hooolly,*" and it felt like a lifetime ago.

Outside, the wind had dropped a little. It was too cloudy for stars, and the lights of the circus were gone. Only the street lights remained. Betsy zigzagged, sticking to the darker spaces between them, and put up her hood to hide her telltale hair.

As she drew level with the vans, she could make out the shadows of stagehands moving among them, shifting shadow-shapes into trailers – all sorts and sizes of crates and boxes and poles and ropes. The performers' trailers were all hitched up to cars too, waiting in lines to leave; their windows were dark and their curtains closed. They were all fast asleep.

Betsy snaked between the trees that ran alongside the line of trailers – some for living in, and others long windowless trailers full of props and set – trying to find Fry's trailer. But instead she found Fry himself. She heard his great voice first, shouting, "Boris!" and quickly scurried behind a tree.

"Boris!" Fry shouted a second time, even though the shadow called Boris was already hurrying over to him. "Take these with the rest of the props," he said, holding out a box. "I can't sleep. They won't

shut up." And Betsy could hear them now – forty-four voices raised in one constant, very annoying chorus of alarm. She smiled.

"I'm trusting you, Boris. If they aren't in the trailer when we arrive..."

"Safe with me, boss."

"They'd better be," Fry said. "Well, since I'm still awake, tell all stagehands to come to my trailer for a quick debrief when you're done here. I might make a couple of changes to the plans, I think. Will you be much longer?"

"Only a few minutes, boss," said the shadow called Boris. And he went tramping off to put the case in the trailer while Fry marched the other way. Betsy counted to five, then peered round the tree to see where Boris went. She watched, helplessly, as he opened a trailer door and disappeared inside. At least she knew where they were now. She just had to wait for the stagehands to finish packing and leave.

It seemed as though it took an age for the last shadow-thing to be packed in to the last shadow-trailer, but eventually it was done. Chuckling among themselves about some joke Betsy hadn't heard, the stagehands ambled off to meet Fry.

Betsy crept out from behind her tree. She ran across the mud, slipping and sliding and only just remaining upright, until she reached the trailer.

It was shut but not locked. She tugged the

door open and slipped inside, shutting it as quietly as possible.

The dark inside the trailer was much darker than the common. Betsy had bumped into three unknown objects within the first three seconds. "*Oh, ow, ooh*," she breathed.

Squeak?

"Oh," she whispered, "where did that come from? Squeak again!"

This time there was a lot more squeaking, from somewhere at the back of the trailer. Betsy inched forwards, her arms stretched out in front of her, in the direction of the squeaks. After much climbing on to and over things, she reached the back of the van.

When she knew she was right by the mice, she put out a hand. No, not *that*, that was something silky – not *that*, it was cold metal –

then her hand met leather.

"Hello!" she whispered.

The squeaks pealed joyfully.

Just then, there were voices and footsteps: the stagehands were back. Betsy froze.

"OK, last checks!" someone called.

There were some muffled thuds. Then the footsteps came closer and someone opened the door of the trailer – only a crack – letting in a slice of the not-quite-dark darkness. Betsy held her breath. Then the door was shut again, and Boris's voice said, "Oops, forgot to lock this one! Don't tell Fry!"

The footsteps left the door and trudged off round the side of the trailer. Betsy breathed out. She listened until the voices and footsteps had stopped again, then forced herself to count out a minute before leaving, to be safe.

Then she would clamber back over everything and make a run for it.

But she had only got as far as five seconds when a thud jolted the whole trailer. It was followed by a *thrummmm.*

The mice stopped mid-squeak, listening. They didn't know what *thrummmm* meant.

Betsy knew and, throwing caution to the wind, she hammered on the side of the trailer, yelling and yelling. But no one could hear her. There was a lurch as the car made its treacly way over the common towards the road, pulling the trailer behind.

Betsy felt when the mud changed to tarmac; she felt the car pick up speed; she knew, thanks to a particularly sickening lurch, when they turned the corner at the end of her road and began the long journey out of London. She didn't give up banging and yelling until they had lurched round ten more corners and were well and truly on their way; then she finally accepted that nobody could hear her.

"Oh, what do I do? What do I do?" she asked the mice.

But there was nothing she *could* do. Just like her grandma before her, Betsy Bow-Linnet was running away with the circus.

OUR EIGHTH ACT

The Accidental Runaway!

The mice enjoyed the journey. Betsy fed them pumpkin seeds galore, and they seemed to find the thrumming of the engine soothing. One by one, they drifted into a contented snooze.

Betsy did not enjoy it.

They drove for hours and hours: it was the longest night she had ever known. She was so frantic worrying about her family, and how she could get home before they found her missing, that at first she didn't notice how hungry and tired and cold she was. But as the hours wore on, she noticed it more and more. She found an enormous padded chicken costume and put that on over her coat, which stopped her shivering. But there wasn't much she could do about the rest.

"Let's get near to the door," she said to the mice, in her best determined voice. "Ready to make a run for it when they open it. We must be nearly there – we've been driving for hours." But only F-to-F-sharp-first-octave was awake to hear this. He pressed his nose to the glass, and blinked.

Flapping her chicken wings, Betsy scrambled back over the props and wedged herself in by the door. She let F-to-F-sharp out and he went scurrying up into her hair, tickling at her ears with his whiskers. His limp was almost gone.

"Hello, trouble," she whispered. "He didn't hurt you?"

The mouse nibbled her ear slightly. He didn't *seem* hurt.

"Hold on tight," Betsy murmured to him – but more to herself really. "We're going to run away from this circus as fast as we can. Then I'll work out how to get us home."

She stayed in a squat, ready to spring, with the case of mice tucked under one elbow. But still the trailer thrummed and thrummed, and no one came to open the doors. Slowly, the squat became more of a squat-sit, and then just a sit; and by the time there was a grey light seeping through the cracks of the door, it was a slump, and Betsy Bow-Linnet was asleep.

She must have slept for a long time. The next thing she knew, the light was strong, the trailer had come to a halt and somebody was lifting something from her wings.

"Five more minutes," she protested.

"What," hissed the somebody, "are *you* doing here?" And although it was only a hiss, it felt like a shout. Betsy opened her eyes to see a frown, alarmingly close. She could see every little whorl and crevice of it: it looked like a very annoyed canyon.

Her brain caught up. It was Chester Fry. And he had her mice.

She sat up quickly and stumbled to her feet and out of the trailer. They were in a strange field with an unknown road winding past and no buildings in sight. The field was bare and empty besides a few stagehands, who were beginning to heave out poles and ropes. The big FRY AND SONS sign was leaning against a nearby trailer, but for now all the bulbs were off, and it didn't look even a little bit magical.

"Goodness me!" boomed Chester, loud enough for the stagehands to hear. "Betsy! I *told* you I couldn't possibly allow a child to work for my circus, and that's my last word." He began

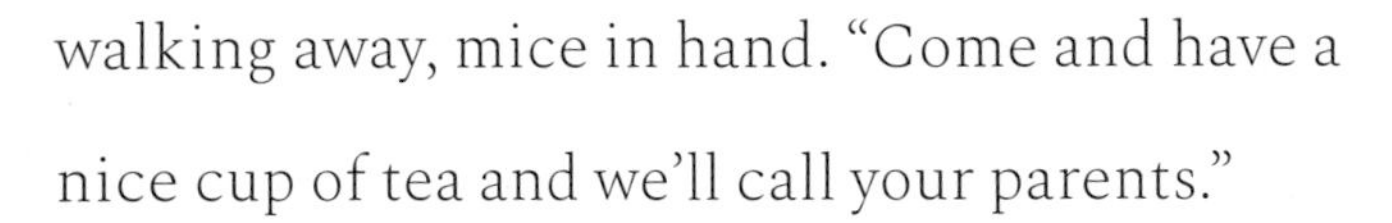

walking away, mice in hand. "Come and have a nice cup of tea and we'll call your parents."

"My mice—" Betsy stumbled after him across the strange field, frantic not to lose sight of the case. She dimly registered that one of the stagehands was sitting down on a stump to eat his lunch. How long had she slept?

"They're perfectly well," said Fry. "Come along. Your parents must be frantic with worry. Why are you dressed as a chicken?" He took the mice into his trailer, so Betsy followed, trying desperately to kick-start her brain while keeping up with him in her chicken outfit.

With the door shut, Fry dropped the act. "I told you," he spat, "to stay away."

"I want my mice—"

"And I want to look after my circus. I do whatever it takes, and I never fail. A word to the wise, Betsy: your grandma was no match for me, and you won't be either."

So he *did* recognize her. Betsy didn't know what he meant by that last bit, but right now she didn't care. She lunged for the mice, but Fry held them easily out of reach.

"However," he went on, "you *are* a nuisance,

I'll give you that. I'll have to pack you off on a train to London. But I have a lot to do today." He considered this, mice aloft, frown deepened in thought. "I have to go into town first, I can't delay. Then I'll get you out of here."

"I'm not leaving without the mice."

"Yes," said Fry, "you are. I suggest you get used to it." And with Betsy still waving her chicken wings in useless protest, he marched out of the trailer with the mice and shut the door before Betsy could reach it. She heard him lock it.

For ten long seconds, she just stood and stared, hoping it was all a dream. But even though she was still half asleep, she knew in her gut that it *wasn't* a dream.

"Oh," she said to F-to-F-sharp, "what do I do? What do I do?"

But F-to-F-sharp had fallen asleep behind her ear.

She sank to the floor and put her head in her wings. Slowly, her brain was coming back to life. She must have slept for hours: her family would have found her empty bed ages ago, and they'd be frantic. *And* the mice were gone. She and F-to-F-sharp were on their own, and she had no idea where they were.

Betsy kept her head in her hands for several long minutes. She took a lot of shaky breaths and told herself to stay calm and roll up her sleeves and put things right: but she wasn't calm, and she couldn't roll up the stupid sleeves of that stupid costume anyway, and she couldn't see how anything could be put right ever.

"I can't fix this," she whispered to the sleeping mouse. "I don't have any more ideas.

I wish I hadn't fallen asleep." She wiped away tears and hugged her knees tightly. "I wish my family were here."

Just then there was a click in the lock.

Betsy turned, every muscle tense, expecting to see Fry. But it was the Splendid who stood in the doorway, twinkling kindly at her over his beard.

"Mr Splendid!" she said. The relief made her tremble all over. "Oh, I'm so happy to see you! I need your help. Please. I have to get back to my family..."

And as though he really was an actually magical magician, who could do actual magical magic, the Splendid drew aside his beard, revealing the doorway behind him: and there, peering past him on the steps, were Bella Bow-Linnet, and Bertram Bow-Linnet, and Grandad.

"Oh!" cried Betsy.

The Splendid winked at her, and twinkled all over.

"Abra," he whispered, "cadabra, Betsy."

OUR NINTH ACT

THE UNTOLD ADVENTURES OF BERYL BOW!

There was no time for explanations. The Splendid hurried her out of Fry's trailer, then all five of them snuck along the back of the line of trailers to the Splendid's home. Only once they were all inside, curtains drawn, could they relax. There wasn't much room, but they made it work, once the Splendid had moved the rabbit and Bertram had folded up his long legs and Grandad had tucked in his elbows.

Bella fell on Betsy in an enormous hug. "Darling," she said, "you must never, ever, ever, ever run off like that again. Ever."

"We were so worried, B," said Bertram. He looked at her with grave disappointment.

"Why don't we hear Betsy's story before we all get in a flap?" said Grandad. "I still think there's more to it than meets the eye. For a start, B, I want to know why you're dressed as a chicken."

"I didn't mean to run away, I promise," said Betsy. "How did you find me?"

"Well, when your bed was empty and we found this –" Grandad held up the bag with Grandma's cloak in, and Betsy realized she had forgotten to put it back – "we had our suspicions. Then when the *Natter* came through our door first thing –" and he wagged an elbow at Bella, who produced a copy from her bag and unrolled it – "we got on the first train down to Higgit-on-Sea."

So that's where they were – wherever that was. Betsy looked at the page that the *Natter* had been opened to. TINY MICE WOW CIRCUS CROWD, it read.

"Oh," she said.

"Luckily," said the Splendid, "I saw you and Fry leave the trailer from my window, so I knew where you were, and I was just out here wondering what to do about it when your family arrived. And I'm a dab hand at picking locks – every magician knows a little escapology. Now I have assured your family that I do not believe you intended to run away with us. Mr Fry told us all you had sold your little mice to the circus."

"I did *not*!" cried Betsy.

"Then spill the beans, B," said Grandad. "What *did* happen? We're listening."

So Betsy took a deep breath and tried to think about where to start. She didn't *want* to start: she wanted to scrub the whole thing out and begin again. But it was too late now – everyone was waiting and Grandad was waggling his elbows in encouragement. So she began.

One way or another, she told it all. She kept interrupting herself to say how sorry she was, and there was a minute of confusion in the middle when F-to-F-sharp woke up and ran off to try nibbling the Splendid's beard, but she got there in the end. And when she had finished, nobody shouted or cried or shook their elbows angrily. Instead, they all tried to hug her at once, which caused a bit of a kerfuffle. Bertram's glasses got knocked off in the confusion and he ended up hugging the Splendid's beard by mistake, but nobody really minded.

When they had all settled back down again, Betsy and Bella were still entwined tightly round each other.

"Oh, Betsy, you should have *told* us," said Bella.

"I didn't want to upset you. After Grandma..."

"I think," said Grandad, "it might be time to talk about your grandma. Perhaps this could all have been avoided if *I* had told *you* a little more, B, instead of avoiding all your questions." He smiled at Betsy. "Enoch is quite right, you know: you *are* the spitting image of her. And I couldn't be more proud."

This was thoroughly muddling. "But ... she made you so unhappy..."

"Come back to me when you've lived to be eighty-three years old, young lady," said Grandad, "and if you've never made anybody unhappy, I'll give you a medal." And his elbows slowed thoughtfully, as he tried to persuade a lifetime of feelings to line up into sentences. Then he took a deep breath and began.

"We made each *other* unhappy," he said. "We loved each other, but we weren't very good for each other somehow. And you have to remember, B, that her whole life – her family, her friends, everything she had ever known since she was a baby girl – was here in the circus. She tried to build a new life with me, and it was a brave and beautiful effort, and I will always be glad we tried."

He smiled sadly at Bella. "She tried extra hard for you, Bells. But it tore her apart. The happy Beryl I knew was already gone, long before she left us." He sighed. "Yes, she hurt us. But I'm not angry with her, B. Not any more.

"*And*," he went on, with a waggle of his finger, "furthermore, that is not her only story. There are many, many more stories that you should know about your grandma. A lifetime of stories. In some of them, she is loyal and brave. She stood up to Chester Fry, for starters, when he betrayed her friends. He never forgave her for that."

Betsy thought of Grandad's letter from Fry – the one in his study. That letter had talked about betrayal, and she had assumed the betrayal was Grandma's. Had she been wrong? Had her grandma been brave, after all?

"Please," she said, "I'd really like to hear that story."

Grandad looked at the Splendid. "Shall I tell it, Enoch, or will you?"

All the twinkle seemed to have gone out of the Splendid. He looked tired. "Perhaps I should tell the *before*," he said, "if you would be so good as to tell the *after*." And Grandad nodded, so the Splendid cleared his throat, and tugged at a piece of beard with each hand for courage, and told his story.

"It happened when Chester took over the circus from his father, Arthur Fry. Arthur Fry was a wonderful man – his circus was more a family than a business. But when he passed away and Chester took the reins on his first night, he dismissed half the performers. To save money, he said. People had lived in this circus their whole lives. Their families had been here for generations. It was our *home*.

"Well, your grandma was furious. She said that if they went, she would go too. She wanted everyone to say the same thing. If we *all* threatened to go, she said, Chester would have to give in.

"It was a long, long night, Betsy. I don't think any of us slept. We had all signed contracts with Fry and we knew that if we broke those, Chester could easily blacken our names with every other circus. No one else would take us. And circus life was all we knew. The risk was enormous.

"So, to cut a long story down to a short and sorry one, most of us let your grandma down. She was dismissed with the others." The Splendid sighed a magnificent sigh, sending ripples down the length of his beard. "Which is, I believe, where you can pick up the story," he said to Grandad.

"Not for another year," said Grandad. "Not until she was almost broken, and she finally turned up on my doorstep to ask for help. You were away, Bells, playing on tour with one of your youth music thingies. She stayed with me for two weeks. We talked about everything – the lives we'd lived, the things we'd learned."

There was a faraway look in Grandad's eyes; Betsy felt a powerful urge to hang on to him, in case he floated away with his memories. "Then," he said, grinning, "we hatched a plan. She was a great plan-hatcher, your grandma. Since no circus would have her, she started her

own travelling show with her animals. It was hard, but she did it – because you could never *completely* break your grandma, B. She was made of something strong." He smiled at his granddaughter. "*That's* why you two are so alike."

There was a moment's silence while Betsy digested all of this. So it was *Fry's* betrayal that Grandad had written a letter about. She and Bella were still hugging very tightly and she could feel her mother's shaky breaths. She wondered whether Grandad had ever told *her* all this before.

Then Grandad leaned forwards and all of his wrinkles arranged themselves into something warlike and fierce. "It is also," he said, "why we will not, under any circumstances, now or ever, be beaten by Chester Fry. Those mice are coming home with us!"

"Of course they are," said Bella. Her voice was a bit wobbly, but fierce too; she sounded a bit like Betsy, and maybe a bit like Grandma. "Let's go and demand them back right now."

"If I may," said the Splendid sadly. "I think demands are unlikely to work. Chester claims he bought them: it's Betsy's word against his. And everybody here will be too afraid to risk siding with Betsy... Afraid of Fry's temper;

afraid of the circus closing if we don't keep those magical mice..."

"Beryl already learned that lesson the hard way," said Grandad. "This family is not going to reason with Chester Fry a second time. We're just going to take the mice and go."

"But," said Betsy, "I don't know where they are."

"And I doubt anybody *will* know, until they're onstage," said the Splendid. "Chester will be spooked when he comes back and finds you're gone – he won't be leaving the mice lying around. I'm afraid we will have to be much sneakier than that, my dear Bow-Linnets."

"Sneaky it is then," said Grandad, and his head thrust forwards into Thinking Position. "*Think*, everyone."

"If we're going to think," said Bertram, in his

most definite voice, "then we'll need these." And he produced a bag full of silver-foil parcels, and the silver-foil parcels were full of cream cakes. Betsy felt about twenty times better just *looking* at them. She scrambled over to hug her father, and took four eclairs for starters.

Then they all sat and ate their cakes, and *thought*. Betsy felt a little more sane with every bite, but she wasn't getting any closer to a plan. Her brain was still whirling from everything Grandad and the Splendid had told her. A hundred questions about her grandma, which she had always pushed away, came flooding in. She, Betsy, was like her grandma. And that was a good thing.

And then the idea came to her. It appeared very suddenly, simple and complete, as though it had been passed to her by ghostly hands.

"Mr Splendid," she said, "you said that the mice will be hidden *until they're onstage*. Can I do my grandma's old vanishing cabinet act with you and get onstage with them that way?"

The Splendid became more twinkle than man at this idea. "But of *course*." He paused, and the twinkle dimmed slightly. "Then what?"

Betsy's mind was whirring now. "Then I do the act, I guess," she said. "Fry can't wrestle the mice off me during the show. I'll head out through the audience quickly when I'm done."

The Splendid nodded slowly, thinking this through. "We may need to delay Fry. The clowns have a bucket on a rope at the top of the big top, which they use to gunk each other. I could perhaps slow Chester down with a little gunk, when your act is finished." (His twinkle definitely brightened at this.)

"And we'll help! We'll be there to stop him!" said Grandad.

"My dear friend, you'll never get inside. Chester sells the tickets himself. He'll remember you. And *you,*" he said to Bella, "look too much like Beryl and Betsy, I'm afraid."

"Then get us in as musicians," said Grandad. "Tell the band we're here to play for Betsy. There's a keyboard, right? Bella, you remember your mother's theme tune?"

"Of course!" Bella's smile curled up her whole face. "You and I used to play it together."

"There we go," said Grandad. "You gunk him, Enoch, and if he recovers too quickly, we'll be at the ringside, ready to get involved. We'll see that you get out of that tent, B."

"But then," said the Splendid, "she'll be in the field, which is not much of an improvement."

Betsy had already been thinking about this. "We need a getaway car. Could we steal Fry's? Just to get us to the station, then we can leave it behind?"

"Stealing a car is complicated, B," said Grandad. "If you don't have the keys to make it drive, you have to be able to hotwire it to make it start … which I doubt anyone here knows about…"

Bertram coughed awkwardly. Everyone looked at him in surprise, except Bella, who looked at him with a knowing smile.

"Er," he said, "I used to, ah, borrow my parents' car sometimes..."

"*Dad!*" said Betsy. First, Grandma was a loyal friend, now Bertram knew how to steal a car. It was turning into a thoroughly muddling day.

"Your father was quite the rebel, Betsy," said Bella. "Back when he was young."

Bertram chewed his cream cake sheepishly and smiled at her. But there was no time to think about her rebel dad. Grandad had taken the news in his stride and was already recapping where everyone needed to be and when. They all had to focus.

Then Betsy thought of something, and it was the sort of thought that twisted up her insides. "Mr Splendid," she said. "Are you sure about this? Won't you be fired?"

"Oh, Fry's been threatening to fire me for

years," said the Splendid. "I'm going to have to let him do it at some point."

"But—"

"No buts, Betsy," he said sternly. "I let my dearest friend down. I have no intention of making the same mistake with her granddaughter." He smiled, and it was a mischievous smile, which made his beard wriggle and dance. "No, not this time. It's time to settle some old scores with Mr Chester Fry."

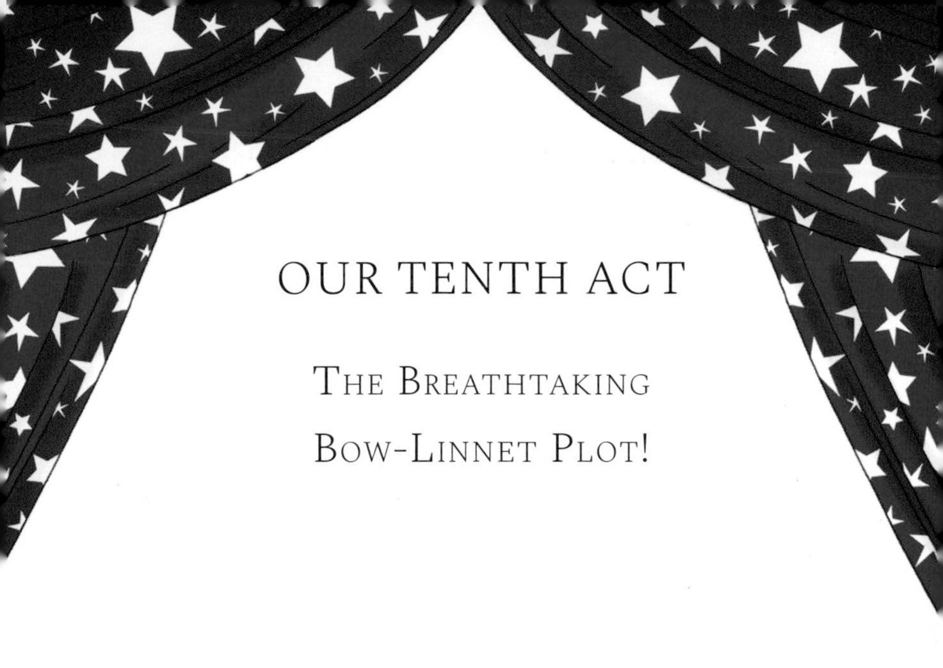

OUR TENTH ACT

The Breathtaking Bow-Linnet Plot!

They waited until the field was thick with an excited crowd and Fry was busy selling tickets on the other side of the tent. Then the Splendid began to sneak in Bow-Linnets.

First, he took Bella and Grandad, to introduce them to the musicians, and Betsy and Bertram stayed behind in his trailer. While he was gone, Betsy took off the chicken suit and her coat and put on the cloak. She was still in her muddy pyjamas, but there was nothing she could do about that now. She gave it a swirl for luck.

"Beautiful, B," said Bertram. Then, as though *he* was a magician, he produced a flower from the sleeve of his jumper. "I was wondering," he said, "if Miss Betsy Bow-Linnet would do me the honour of wearing this flower for her performance tonight."

It was an old tradition between the two of them, but Betsy hadn't expected it now.

"Wait," she said, "when did you get hold of a flower?"

But Bertram just winked and tucked it in her hair.

Then, when the performers started milling about and knocking on each other's doors, Bertram slipped away from the Splendid's trailer. He went to the far end of the field to stand about casually and look like a man who would never dream of stealing a car – which was not difficult, actually.

As for Betsy, the vanishing cabinet stood waiting in the centre of the room. The ostrich had been banished to a corner of the trailer, where it stood looking woeful. The Splendid showed Betsy the secret compartment in the side that looked like a wall, and the bits where you could stick swords through to be extra impressive. When he had promised her that there would be no swords tonight, impressive or otherwise, she squeezed inside.

"Comfortable, Betsy?"

"*Nggh,*" said Betsy in reply.

"I must apologize. It's not normally necessary to be in there for more than a few moments. I do hope you can find an acceptable position."

"*Nggh,*" she explained.

"Very good then," said the Splendid. "I shall wheel you over. Please vanish all sounds, Betsy, to complete the illusion."

So Betsy was silent, as was F-to-F-sharp, who

was behaving himself very well. He seemed impressed by the secretive darkness of the vanishing cabinet, and was keeping very still just above Betsy's left ear.

With a rattle-*bump*, the Splendid lifted the cabinet down the trailer steps and wheeled it across the grass to the big top.

They glided through the curtains into the wings. No one stopped them. Then the Splendid parked the cabinet and, with a goodbye tap, he left.

For a few minutes, girl and mouse waited in cramped silence. Then the show began.

First, Betsy had seen the show from the seats. Then she had seen it from the trailer steps and the stage itself. Now she was hidden right in its heart. She felt the muffled beat of the music like a pulse. The show became a series of hurrying feet running for their cue; hasty good-luck rituals between the performers before they went onstage together; and whispered congratulations or complaints as they came back off again. She heard an acrobat curse his weak ankle, and Fry chivvying people, and a clown complaining that her act would have been much funnier if someone hadn't lost the chicken costume.

From another world, she heard the waves of applause around the ring. It was hard to believe that only two days ago she had sat there and applauded until her hands hurt. Speaking of which, pretty much *everything* hurt right now. Very, very gently, she adjusted her position.

At last the wait was over and Betsy felt herself being wheeled onstage as Fry announced the Splendid's act. Betsy could tell by the faint chittering nearby that she had been put right next to the mice, who were waiting on the magician's table. Frantic, F-to-F-sharp pressed his nose to the wall, tiny heart pounding against the side of Betsy's neck.

"Shhh," she whispered. "Soon. Soon."

There were *oohs* and *aahs* as the Splendid vanished things and unvanished them again in increasingly unlikely ways. Then, at last, she heard him announcing his final trick. There were thuds and bumps as he showed the audience the cabinet, cleverly distracting their attention from the real hiding place.

"And now," he said, "I must wish you goodbye! *Abraaaacadabraaaa!*" A drum rolled. He stepped inside. He and Betsy switched places in a confusion of limbs. The drum roll stopped.

There was a ting from the cymbal, and Betsy

stepped out, smiling, arms aloft.

There was a ripple of surprised and delighted laughter, then everyone applauded. Fry had stepped into the ring, smile wide. When he saw Betsy, his smile vanished like a magic trick, and he turned the same colour as his jacket with astonishing speed. Betsy had to fight a sudden wild urge to laugh.

She opened the cabinet to reveal the Splendid for his final round of applause. Then she put her hands very firmly on the box of mice.

The applause died away and there was an expectant silence.

The audience waited for Fry to announce Betsy. When he rudely failed to do so, Betsy announced herself. Then she said, "Please, ladies and gentlemen, raise your binoculars!" – and she opened the case of mice. "Line up!" They marched into position and with a squeak of delight, F-to-F-sharp ran down to join them. His limp was barely noticeable; maybe, Betsy decided, it was time to let him rejoin his family.

From the band, four clever hands struck up the most joyful dancing music Betsy had ever heard: Grandma's music. The moment it began, Fry's face flushed even deeper red. Betsy looked round at her mother and grandfather, who were grinning at each other as they played, their fingers doing the work all by themselves as they flew through this tune they knew so well. Grandad even found time to wave at Fry between notes.

Then Betsy and the mice began.

It didn't feel as easy as last time. Nothing feels easy when you're being glowered at by a tomato in a suit, whose fingers are curling in and out as though they'd like to squash forty-four very tiny mice and one small girl. But the mice performed perfectly, paws pattering smartly through their routine, and the crowd loved them.

The music helped. Betsy focused on that and tried to ignore Fry. But when the time came for their bow, she felt feverish with nerves.

"Bow!" she called extra loudly, to make certain the Splendid couldn't miss it. And sure enough, right on cue, a magnificent stream of gunk and glitter came tumbling down from the rig and gushed over Fry. With a roar, he took a step forwards, and immediately slipped and fell. The audience went nuts.

There was no time to enjoy the applause. Betsy called the mice back into their case and took off while Fry struggled to remove his impossibly slippery shoes. Between the gunk and the glitter, he looked like an unusually angry Christmas tree.

But the gunk had spattered far and wide when it fell and on her way to the ringside, Betsy slipped too. By the time she was up and running again, Fry had recovered and raced ahead of her to block off the aisle. He reached out his hands.

"*Yaaaaaaaah!*" yelled somebody (because battle cries are a family thing) and to Betsy's astonishment, Bella came flying through the air on the end of a rope. She unfurled one leg as she flew, and it met Fry squarely on the shoulder, sending him skidding back on to the floor.

The audience were beside themselves. This was the best circus ever.

Betsy seized the moment to start running up the aisle. She heard Fry staggering to his feet, but she didn't look round. She didn't even look round when she heard Grandad saying, "Oh no you *don't*," and the unmistakable squelch of someone being pied in the face with extraordinary vim. She kept going, back down the steps on the other side, under the seats, and out into the cold night air. Then she was racing towards the waiting car headlights, the mice safely in her hands, her heart soaring.

She was so busy running and heart-soaring, she didn't register the ring of shadows all round the car until she had run right up to it.

It was the stagehands. They were waiting for her.

THE FINAL ACT

Mr Fry's Scandalous Secrets

The stagehands had wrestled the mice back by the time Fry, Grandad and Bella came panting up behind Betsy. They were in Boris's clutches once more, and he hugged them protectively, muscles bulging. From the car, Bertram looked out nervously. For some reason, the windscreen wipers were waving back and forth at top speed.

"What *now*? Why is that man in my car?" roared Fry. The glitter on his nose and jowls trembled. The stagehands shifted nervously, and explained that he had stolen it, and they hadn't noticed, and they were very sorry, but they had managed to clamp it as soon as he stopped, and so everything was all right now, really.

"Why," bellowed Fry, "are the wipers on?"

The stagehands looked at each other. Boris gestured for Bertram to wind down the window. "Oi," he said, "what's up with the wipers?"

Bertram looked a bit sheepish. "Can't seem to make them stop. Er, possible I damaged something... Sorry, I haven't done this in a while. Hello, Betsy."

"Hello, Dad."

"Hello, you two."

"Hello, darling."

"Hello, Ber—"

"ENOUGH!" shouted Fry. "Please have your touching family reunions later."

"Aren't *you* going to say hello to me, Chester?" asked Grandad. "It's been a long time."

By now, most of the circus performers had

come out to see what was happening, the Splendid at the helm.

"What's going on, Fry?" said the strongwoman.

"Trespass and theft is what's going on," spat Fry.

"It's not theft," said Betsy. "They're *mine.*"

"And might I suggest," said the Splendid, "that it's not really trespass either, Chester. Nobody belongs in this circus more than the granddaughter of our own Gloria Sprightly."

There was a murmur of surprise and approval. Betsy felt a glow of pride that her grandma's name could have that effect, even among performers who had never known her. Obviously she was still talked about.

By now, the audience were beginning to trickle out from the tent, and some of the nosiest came to see what all the fuss was about. Betsy drew herself up as tall and proud as she could, rippling her grandma's cloak, and turned to Boris. "I would like," she said, "my mice back."

Boris looked at Fry.

"The mice are the property of the circus," said Fry. He looked as determined as a man covered in gunk can look. The audience stared at Fry, then Betsy, then Fry: it was his word against hers.

"You must know that's not true," said Betsy, appealing to the performers. "Don't believe him!"

"It's balderdash! It's poppycock!" agreed the Splendid. He waved a fist, which was overdoing it a bit, but Betsy appreciated the support.

"They do not know any such thing, young

lady," Fry declared. "I bought those mice fair and square. What they *do* know is where their loyalties lie."

The circus performers exchanged uneasy glances. There was a moment of deafening silence, as everybody hoped that somebody else would take the lead. The audience waited eagerly. The *swish-thud* of the wipers was the only sound.

"And they *know*," Fry pressed on, "that these mice – *our* mice – are crucial to this circus. Without them, I cannot afford to keep our family together." And from the way he glared at them all, it was quite clear that the first to speak would be the first to find themselves suddenly unaffordable.

("Ahem," said Bertram. But no one heard.)

"But Fry," began the strongwoman, in her

most sensible voice. Fry shot her a look of such poison that she faltered.

("Er," said Bertram. But it was lost under the swooshing of the windscreen wipers.)

"Please," said Betsy, "help me. You know I would never sell my mice. They're *mine*."

"I agree!" shouted the Splendid excitedly. "I agree! Fire me! I stand with Beryl – er, Betsy!"

("Ahem," said Bertram, really quite loudly this time.)

There was a murmuring among the performers and a few started to mutter that really they did think that actually the mice were Betsy's. The strongwoman folded her arms, and announced, "She's right. Those mice are hers, Fry."

But others were still uneasy. "We need them," Betsy heard.

"We've got to make ends meet."

"We lost Seraphina. Fair's fair."

Boris looked thoroughly confused, but he clutched the mice tighter.

The Splendid was by now beside himself with excitement, and climbed on the roof of the car to start a speech; but before he could get started, Bertram leaned right out of the car window and AHEMMMED so loudly

that it made Betsy jump. Everybody fell silent and looked at him.

"Maybe it's not relevant," he said, "but since you're so short of money, I thought you might be interested to know that there's an awful lot in the glove compartment of this car."

Even under all the gunk and glitter, Betsy could see that Fry turned pale. The performers stared at Bertram with wide eyes and open mouths. There was a moment's absolute silence. Then they turned as one angry beast to Fry.

"Hundreds of pounds in cash," added Bertram. "It's strange. I broke into the car earlier – just to get a feel for it, you know – and it wasn't there then."

"That *is* strange," said the strongwoman. "Because all the takings from the show are *supposed* to go straight in the safe, Fry. So you've been taking some for yourself, have you? Do you do this every night?"

The audience murmured appreciatively. This was even better than the circus.

"Do you mean to tell me," said the acrobat, "that Fry's been making us cut costs just so that he can get rich?"

"You *fired* Joe and Dave and the whole bike team," added a clown, reddening, "and you said it was because we couldn't afford them. But you just wanted more money for yourself, is that it?"

From the roof of the car, the Splendid shook his fist and cried, "I had to ration the rabbit's carrots, you villain!"

"You see!" cried Betsy. Her heart swelled. The tide was turning. "The circus isn't poor at all. It's just a lie to scare you all. Your only problem is Fry. *You* should be firing *him.* You just need to stick together, that's all!"

"Hear! hear!" said Grandad.

"That's right, darling!" said Bella.

Bertram tooted his horn. Someone in the audience cheered, and it spread. The windscreen wipers thudded their approval.

The strongwoman stepped forward. "Give Betsy her mice back, Boris."

Boris looked from Fry, to the strongwoman, to the fierce girl in the velvet cloak, back to Fry. A little uncertainly, he held out the case to Betsy.

The crowd loved it. There was applause and cheering. Boris seemed a bit taken aback and gave an awkward bow.

"Thank you," said the strongwoman. "I resign from Fry's Circus."

"Me too!" cried the Splendid, beard flying in the wind like a flag. "Me too!"

"ME TOO!" said Boris, startling himself. After that, it was a hailstorm of resigning, until there was no one left in Fry's Circus except a glowering pile of gunk.

"We'll be forming our own circus then, Chester," announced the Splendid. "Abracadabra! And I think we might keep the big top and all the trailers and the props. Unless you'd like to go to the police about it, of course, in which case we can discuss the small matter of the money you've been taking..."

Fry made a furious *HMMF* sort of noise, but it wasn't much of a response and he knew it. He was looking a bit dazed by the sudden turn of events. He was still not quite sure what had happened, but he knew who was responsible, and he glowered at the Bow-Linnets furiously.

Everyone entirely ignored his glowering, which made him glower more than ever. He tried shouting at some of the stagehands, but they weren't listening.

Boris removed the clamp from the car. "Sorry about that," he said to Bertram, opening the door for him. He shook his hand, and Betsy's. "If you lot need a lift home tonight, I can take you – I owe you one."

"Thank you," said Betsy. She looked around at the fierce performers, and the rapt crowd, and the twinkling lights, and the glimmering stars overhead, and she didn't know if she had ever felt so happy. "Maybe we could stay?" She looked over to Bella and Grandad. "Just for a little bit?"

"Of course," said Bella. "It seems to *me* like it might be a good time for a little party?"

At the word party, Grandad shuddered. "Lord help us," he said. "Do you know, I think I feel a sudden nap coming on."

CURTAIN CALL

Then it was all a whirl, and Betsy began to lose track. Some of the performers march-hustled a gunk-covered Fry to the edge of the field and wished him a stern farewell. Someone persuaded the musicians to get their instruments back out. Meanwhile, the fire dancer began a bonfire, and somebody else drove off in the car to buy food and drink with that evening's stolen money; and in an astonishingly short time, Betsy was toasting a marshmallow over the fire while the hurdy-gurdy music played.

The Splendid's ostrich had been brought outside and decorated in glitter for the occasion. Everyone was dancing and laughing. Bella was dancing with the Splendid. Grandad was dancing with the strongwoman, elbows twirling, and Bertram was explaining to the fire dancer exactly *how* you go about stealing a car. Betsy watched them all, and she thought her heart might burst.

She bent down to the box at her feet. Her

grandma's deep blue cloak rippled out from her like a river.

"You all right in there?" she asked.

And forty-four tiny acrobats blinked brightly back at her, because they were *always* all right. That's the nice thing about the mice. They were made of something strong, just like Betsy – just like Grandma. F-to-F-sharp was nibbling off his bandage, squeaking happily.

The lights of the big top winked down at her. Betsy smiled back up at them. She was going to miss those lights when the circus went on its way without her.

But that was all right. One day, she would be back.

FRY and SONS'
CIRCUS OF WONDERS

ABOUT THE AUTHOR

Sylvia Bishop spent an entire childhood reading fiction, dreaming up stories and pretending. Now she writes her stories down for a living, preferably by lamp-light with tea. Her first book, *Erica's Elephant*, was published in 2016. She has since written two further titles for young readers, *The Bookshop Girl* and *A Sea of Stories*, and two middle-grade mysteries, *The Secret of the Night Train* and *Trouble in New York*. Her books have been translated into sixteen languages, including French, Dutch, Russian and Japanese.

Find out more at sylviabishopbooks.com.

ABOUT THE ILLUSTRATOR

Ashley King is an illustrator working in leafy Warwickshire. He has a bachelor's degree with honors in Illustration and Animation. He skillfully hand draws all his creations with humour and emotion mixed with a digital twist. Ashley is the illustrator of many children's books, including the *Witch for a Week* series by Kaye Umansky and *The Magical Adventures of Whoops the Wonder Dog* by TV chef Glynn Purnell. This will be the fourth book Ashley has illustrated for Sylvia and he is over the moon to be working on this new series together.

Look out for

44 Tiny Chefs

... coming soon!

When Betsy's dad agrees to bake the cakes for a Royal Gala he has no idea how big a job it is.

As time ticks on Betsy knows the only way he'll get it done is with a little help from her forty-four mice. Just as long as she can keep them away from prying eyes...